This book belongs to

_____

First published in Great Britain by HarperCollins Publishers Ltd in 1995. ISBN 0 00 198160 9 (hardback) 10 9 8 7 6 5 4 3 2 1
ISBN 0 00 664556 9 (paperback) 10 9 8 7 6 5 4 3 2   Text and illustrations copyright © Mark Burgess 1995

Teddy and Rabbit's
Runaway Washing

Mark Burgess

Collins

An Imprint of HarperCollinsPublishers

Teddy and Rabbit were going to
see Mouse.

"I'll just get the umbrella," said Teddy.

"We don't need an umbrella," said
Rabbit. "It's not raining."

"We might," said Teddy. "You
never know."

When they arrived at Mouse's house,
Teddy rang the doorbell.
There was no answer.
"Perhaps Mouse is in the back
garden," said Rabbit.

Teddy and Rabbit bumped into
Mouse running down the path.
"Did you see it?" gasped Mouse.

"What?" asked Teddy.
"My washing," said Mouse. "It's blown away."

"There it is!" shouted Rabbit, excitedly.
The washing was flying away like a kite.

Off ran Teddy, Rabbit and Mouse
after the washing.

But they couldn't catch it.

Then at last the washing caught in
a tree.
"Ah, ha," said Teddy. "It's lucky I
brought the umbrella."
Teddy reached up and then, just as
he was about to unhook the washing...

Away it blew again,

all the way to Elephant's house...

...where the washing tied itself to the flagpole.

"It's quite dry," said Elephant, after he had taken it down.

"Oh, thank you, Elephant," said Mouse. "Now, let's go home and have some tea."

"You'd better hurry," said Elephant.
"It's going to rain."
"It's lucky I brought the umbrella!"
said Teddy.